GREAT ESCAPES

NAZI PRISON CAMP ESCAPE

GREAT ESCAPES

NAZI PRISON CAMP ESCAPE

BY **MICHAEL BURGAN**

EDITED BY **MICHAEL TEITELBAUM**

HARPER

An Imprint of HarperCollins*Publishers*

For my father, a World War II vet
who encouraged my interest in history
and supported my efforts to write about it.

Library of Congress Cataloging-in-Publication Data

Names: Burgan, Michael, author. | Teitelbaum, Michael, compiler.

Title: Nazi prison camp escape / by Michael Burgan ; edited by
Michael Teitelbaum.

Description: First edition. | New York, NY : HarperCollins,
[2020] | Series: Great escapes ; book 1 | Audience: Ages 8–12
| Audience: Grades 4–6 | Summary: "The epic story of William
Ash and the escape from Stalag Luft III German POW camp
during World War II"—Provided by publisher.

Identifiers: LCCN 2019026847 | ISBN 978-0-06-286036-1
(hardcover) | ISBN 978-0-06-286035-4 (paperback)

Subjects: LCSH: Ash, William, 1917–2014—Juvenile literature.
| World War, 1939–1945—Prisoners and prisons, German—
Juvenile literature. | Prisoner-of-war escapes—Germany—
History—20th century—Juvenile literature. | Prisoners of
war—United States—Biography—Juvenile literature. | Stalag
Luft III—Biography—Juvenile literature. | Canada. Royal
Canadian Air Force—Officers—Biography—Juvenile literature.

Classification: LCC D805.G3 B866 2020 | DDC 940.54/7243092—dc23

LC record available at https://lccn.loc.gov/2019026847

Typography by David Curtis

20 21 22 23 24   PC/LSCH   10 9 8 7 6 5 4 3 2 1

❖

First Edition

NOR
SWEDEN
DENMARK
Hamburg
Berlin
Warsaw
Amsterdam
NETHERLANDS
NAZI
GERMANY
Stalag Luft III
Sagan
Leipzig
Breslau
Brussels
BELGIUM
Dulag Luft
Auschwitz
LUX.
Prague
Nuremberg
aris
CZECH
REPUBLIC
Vienna
Munich
RANCE
HUNGARY
SWITZERLAND
YUGOSLAVIA
Milan
ITALY

Chapter One

THE FIRST TRY

On a summer morning in 1942, Bill Ash joined the other prisoners trudging across the sandy ground toward a small concrete building. The men were being held at a German prisoner-of-war (POW) camp called Stalag Luft III. Now they were supposed to take their weekly hot shower. But Ash and his friend Paddy Barthropp had other plans.

Ash had arrived at Stalag Luft III just a few weeks before, in early June. The camp, located outside Sagan, Germany, was built in April of that year, and the Germans considered it escape-proof. *We'll see about that*, Ash had thought when he first heard that claim. To Ash and most of the other prisoners, trying to escape was part of their duty as military officers. There was no other choice. Ash was not planning to spend the rest of the war rotting in this place. He had decided his weekly shower was going to give him a chance to win his freedom.

"Are you ready?" Ash whispered to Barthropp, who walked next to him. The blond-haired pilot nodded. He and Ash had arrived at Stalag Luft III together, and now they would leave together—if their escape went according to plan.

The two friends had traveled different paths to end up together as prisoners of war. Barthropp, the son of a wealthy British family, had joined Great Britain's Royal Air Force (the RAF) before the war began. Ash, a poor, twenty-four-year-old Texan, had volunteered to fight, first for Canada then for the British, once the war broke out. Despite their different backgrounds, Ash knew that he and Barthropp had a lot in common. They both loved the thrill of flying fighter planes at more than 350 miles per hour. They both hated the

Nazis, who had taken control of Germany, and the war they had started to try to take over most of Europe. And perhaps most importantly, the two were ready to risk their lives rather than let the Nazis keep them imprisoned.

Ash kept his head down as he followed the other prisoners into the concrete building. They showered together, standing in a large open space under the faucets that lined the wall. The Germans gave the men a short burst of water, time to soap up, and then a second blast of water to rinse.

Ash and Barthropp joined the others in taking off their clothes. But instead of taking a shower, while the guards waited outside, the two men made their way to a trapdoor in the floor. The door led to a small space that contained the valves for turning off the main water supply to the showers. Ash had noticed the door several weeks earlier, and it gave him an idea.

"We can hide in that space beneath the trapdoor," he had told Barthropp. "The other men can distract the goons so they can't get a good head count after the shower. That way, they won't miss us while we hide. Then at night, we can sneak out of the shower building, cut the barbed wire, and run to freedom."

Fearing escape attempts, the German guards, called "goons" by the prisoners, always counted the number of prisoners both before and after each shower to make sure no one was missing.

"I like it," Barthropp had said with a nod. "But will the escape committee?"

Because the prisoners of Stalag Luft III had plenty of free time and opportunities to meet, they had the chance to create a committee to review any escape plan. These officers had to give their okay for the plan to go forward. If the committee approved, they helped the men with food, maps, and other supplies. When Ash and Barthropp told the committee about their plan, the officers agreed to support it. Now, Ash and Barthropp had to put their plan into action.

They knew escaping would not be easy. The Germans built Stalag Luft III in an isolated spot, as far as possible from neighboring Poland, so no one there could help an escaping prisoner. Two separate barbed-wire fences surrounded the camp. Guards armed with machine guns stood in towers along the fences. Other towers held spotlights that could light almost every corner of the camp as if it were daytime. Just beyond the outer fence, specially trained guards patrolled, looking for signs of an escape attempt. The prisoners nicknamed them "ferrets." Their job was to ferret out, or look for, possible escapees. But Ash couldn't worry about those obstacles now. He had to focus on the first part of his escape plan.

As the shower room filled with steam, he and Barthropp lifted the trapdoor and climbed down into their hiding place. Above them, they heard the voices of the prisoners. Then, one voice rose up above the others. One of the prisoners was shouting at the guards.

"What are they doing up there?" Ash whispered. Barthropp, his face tightening with nerves, could only shrug. The plan was for the other men to cause a disturbance *after* the shower. That

way the goons would miscount the men as they returned to their barracks. The hope was that they wouldn't notice that Ash and Barthropp were missing. But it sounded like someone was stirring up trouble too soon.

"Your Hitler is a rat-faced jerk!" the prisoner shouted. "If I get out of here, I hope I can kill him with my bare hands."

Ash heard a guard yelling back in German, telling the prisoner to shut up. But he went on, calling Adolf Hitler, Germany's leader, other names. More voices joined in the shouting, and then Ash heard shuffling feet.

"The goons are taking them out now," Ash said. "Before they can rinse."

"I hope the men can still keep them from getting a good count," Barthropp whispered.

Several minutes passed. To Ash, it seemed like hours. He tried to take deep breaths and remain calm in his cramped hiding spot. Then, the two men heard the howl of sirens.

"That's trouble," Ash hissed. "They know we're missing."

Assuming they were going to be caught, the two men quickly ripped up the hand-drawn map the escape committee had given them.

"The food too," Ash said softly. He began shoving the food they had brought for their escape into his mouth. Barthropp did too, so the Germans wouldn't get it. The prisoners called it "the Mixture"—a blend of chocolate and foods the men had collected, such as oats and fruit that had been boiled and dried. The Mixture was easy to carry and provided the nutrition they needed during an escape.

As Ash and Barthropp frantically ate, they heard footsteps right above them. *The guards*, Ash thought. *Please don't find the trapdoor!* Then Ash heard the growling of the camp's ferocious German shepherds. A few seconds later, Ash saw the door above him fling open. He looked up to see several rifles pointing down and the snarling dogs straining at their leashes.

Without saying a word, Ash and Barthropp put up their hands. With their faces covered in chocolate from the Mixture, they climbed out of their hiding place. Ash gave one last bit of the Mixture to one of the dogs. He thought, *Maybe he'll think I'm a good guy and leave me alone the next time I try to escape. Because I know one thing: I will try again.*

Chapter Two

FIGHTING THE NAZIS

Bill Ash was nine years old in 1927, when the great pilot Charles Lindbergh came to Bill's hometown of Dallas, Texas.

"Can you see him?" Bill asked his mother. "Is he coming?"

"Not yet, dear. But he will."

"Lucky Lindy," as Lindbergh was called, had just become the first person to fly alone across the Atlantic Ocean. Now, all over the United States, cities were throwing parades to honor this new American hero.

A chilly rain fell on that September afternoon as Bill and his mother joined thousands of others lining the street for the parade. Bill heard a roar sweeping through the crowd. The noise rolled closer to him as Lindbergh approached in an open car. He waved to the thousands of people along the street. Bill joined the crowd in waving back.

"Mr. Lindbergh!" Bill called. "Lucky Lindy! Hello!"

Bill watched as the car slowly inched past. And he thought, *It must be great to be able to fly*.

But after the parade, and during the next few years, young Bill Ash didn't have too much time to think about flying. His family moved from one neighborhood to another in Dallas. His father sold hats for a living and sometimes struggled to pay the rent, so the family moved to find less expensive housing. Bill worked part-time in high school to help pay the bills, and he kept on working through college. During that time, the world was going through the Great Depression. When Bill left college, the world was facing another crisis: war in Europe.

◆◆◆

THE GREAT DEPRESSION

Bill Ash was just one of the millions of Americans affected by the Great Depression. This economic crisis began in October 1929. During the 1920s, many people had bought stock in US companies. The stock made them part owners of the companies. When the companies didn't perform as expected, the value of many stocks began to fall. A great many people tried to sell their stocks all at once, causing a stock market crash. Banks did not have enough money in reserve to pay everyone who wanted to sell their stocks. People lost money, and some who had borrowed money to buy stocks could not pay back what they owed. Many companies also suffered, as people had less to spend on items for their homes or to buy cars. Companies fired workers, who often couldn't find new jobs. By 1933, about 25 percent of Americans were out of work. They struggled to feed their families or find housing they could afford. The Great Depression spread around the world and lasted through the 1930s.

Bill read in the papers about Adolf Hitler and his Nazi Party, who had started the war in Europe by invading Poland in September of 1939. France and Great Britain soon came to Poland's aid. But the Nazis of Germany had built a powerful military force and easily took control of Poland.

Bill saw the danger Germany posed to other democratic nations. He read about how Hitler was locking up Jewish people, who had committed no crimes, in concentration camps. Now Hitler wanted to conquer large parts of Europe. The Allied countries agreed that the war in Europe was fueled by Hitler's desire for power and his hatred of Jews and others he considered less human than Germans.

CONCENTRATION CAMPS

Long before the Nazis built Stalag Luft III and other POW camps, they had set up another type of camp all across Germany. These were called concentration camps, where Adolf Hitler sent anyone who he thought threatened his rule, such as political opponents, and anyone he deemed "inferior."

The worst of these camps were the Nazi's six death camps, where they murdered millions of innocent people for no reason other than that Hitler and the Nazis considered them "racially undesirable." In an attack known as genocide, the Nazis killed six million Jews, at least 1.9 million Poles, and hundreds of thousands of Romany people (who were also known as Gypsies), gay people, people with disabilities, religious officials, and members of political parties that opposed the Nazis.

Before being killed, prisoners in concentration camps first had to work for the Nazis. Some cut trees or dug for minerals in mines, while others constructed roads and buildings, often working fourteen hours a day, seven days a week. Guards watched closely as the prisoners worked, and many soldiers took pleasure in beating the prisoners. Unlike POW camps, concentration camps were not governed by international rules protecting prisoners.

The Nazis' deliberate mass killing of more than six million Jews is known today as the Holocaust. Most of the people who died in the Holocaust were killed by poisonous gas, but some also died from disease and starvation.

But in the summer of 1940, the United States had not yet gotten directly involved in the war. Some Americans even openly supported Hitler. As Bill Ash traveled the country looking for work, he sometimes got into fights over the issue. After one brawl, a bystander called out, "If you hate Hitler so much, why don't you go fight him."

"I just might do that," Bill replied.

Then in 1940, Ash wound up in Detroit. While eating a meal at a diner, he looked at the other young men eating nearby.

"Boys, wish me luck," Ash said. "I'm going to Canada to join the air force and shoot down some Nazis."

The others in the diner laughed. To most

Americans, the war was something that was happening far away and had nothing to do with them. But the young men quieted as they saw Ash leave the diner and start walking to the nearby border with Canada. They realized that he was serious. However, a short time later, Ash returned to the diner.

"Hey, hotshot," one man called out. "How many Nazis did you kill?"

Ash looked down. "They didn't take me," he said. "They said I was too skinny."

Ash borrowed some money, then began to eat as much food as he could. He stuffed himself day after day. Two weeks later, he returned to Canada and tried to volunteer again.

The recruiting sergeant looked him over, then told him to step onto a scale. The sergeant checked his weight.

"Okay," he told Ash. "You're in."

Ash smiled as the others in the room cheered. "Welcome aboard, Yank," someone called out. Fighting for a foreign air force meant Ash had to give up his US passport and citizenship. But he didn't care. All he wanted was to go to Europe, fly planes, and help defeat the Nazis.

Other "Yanks" joined Ash in volunteering for Canada. Although an independent nation, Canada had close ties with Great Britain, and British pilots trained the Canadians and the Americans who volunteered. Like Ash, those Americans wanted to fight Hitler right away, rather than wait to see if the United States entered the war.

As he trained, Ash discovered that he had a natural talent for flying. He also followed the events in Europe. British pilots in the Royal Air Force were heroically battling German planes over the skies of England. When Ash and the others finished their training, they too would fly for the RAF.

Some of the men learning how to fly wondered if the war would even last that long.

"The Germans are dropping so many bombs every day," one young pilot said. "And they just invaded France."

"It doesn't look good," another pilot agreed. "I don't know if we'll be able to stop them."

"Now, don't get so down," Ash said. "The RAF will hold off those Germans, and before you know it, we'll be over there shooting down Nazi planes, too."

As it turned out, Ash was right. The training in Canada soon ended, and he and the others headed to England. In the spring of 1941, Ash climbed into the cockpit of a Spitfire aircraft for the first time. He was about to fly one of the world's best fighter planes.

Ash looked over all the controls. With the touch of a button, he could fire the plane's machine guns at an attacking enemy. Once he was airborne, any fear Ash felt vanished as he guided the powerful aircraft through the skies during his final training missions. *I can do this*, he thought. *I can fly a Spitfire as good as anybody!*

By the fall of 1941, his training was over. Ash finally got a chance to face the Nazis in the air. On his missions, he and other Spitfire pilots often protected ships and slower bomber planes as they headed for their targets. He loved the speed and agility of the Spitfire. *It's like driving a sports car,* he thought—*except for the German guns firing at me from down on the ground.*

When he landed, Ash would check the outside of the plane to see how many times he had been hit but still managed to keep flying. Others, though, were not so lucky. Ash knew plenty of pilots who never made it back alive. For almost six months, Ash flew dangerous missions, always managing to return to his home base in the town of Hornchurch, just outside London.

On March 24, 1942, Ash headed to the airfield for another mission. The mist began to clear, and fighter planes and bombers took off for a target in Belgium. On the way back after a successful run, his radio blared to life.

"Enemy planes closing in!" another pilot warned. Ash made a sharp turn to try to spot them. Within seconds, he was firing his machine guns, watching the bullets rip into a German plane. It fell out of the sky in a cloud of gray smoke.

But more German planes were soon circling around him. Ash aimed at another fighter plane and fired again, but this time his guns jammed.

Then he felt the plane begin to slow. Ash's mind raced. *The engine's been hit—now what do I do?* He could see more German fighters approaching. *Either I bail out, or I crash.*

He knew that floating down to earth with a parachute would make him an easy target for the German guns. As his Spitfire neared the ground, Ash looked for a good place to crash-land. He was flying over France, and he could only hope that once he landed a friendly French citizen would find him before the Germans did.

SPITFIRES AND OTHER AIRCRAFT OF WORLD WAR II

The first practical airplane flew in 1903, and by 1914, when World War I broke out, countries around the world realized planes would be useful in war. They could scout out enemy positions, and pilots could also drop bombs and fire machine guns from the air at troops on the ground. The first military planes were made mostly of wood and strong fabric, and the pilots sat in an open cockpit. Most of the planes had two sets of wings, though some had as many as three, stacked one on top of the other.

As World War I went on, air forces developed a strategy that continued in World War II. Larger planes were equipped with bombs, while faster fighter planes protected them from enemy planes.

The plane Bill Ash flew in World War II, the Spitfire, was one of the best fighter planes made.

By the time World War II started, airplanes were being made of aluminum and most had just one set of wings. Pilots could also talk to each other using radios. Throughout the war, Great Britain kept improving the Spitfire, and by 1943 some models had a top speed of 440 miles per hour and could reach an altitude of 40,000 feet.

Pilots like Ash appreciated how easy it was to fly the Spitfire, and the plane and its pilots were famous for winning many "dogfights" in the air against German airplanes. The Spitfires often confronted German fighter planes called

Messerschmitt Bf 109s.

The Spitfire was a little faster, but the German plane flew better at higher altitudes.

In 1944, Germany produced the most advanced plane of the war—the Messerschmitt Me 262. It was the world's first plane powered by a jet engine and had a top speed of about 540 miles per hour. By the time these planes first saw action, however, Germany was starting to lose the war. US and British bombers were able to destroy some of the jet fighters while they were still on the ground. By the war's end, some British bombers could carry up to eleven tons of bombs on one flight.

Chapter Three

HIDING

Ash peered out his cockpit window and saw that he was quickly descending. The roof of a church below raced toward him as he stared out the window. "Better not hit that," he said out loud, and he tilted the plane so that one wing would dig into the ground.

The Spitfire touched down and began to do cartwheels. Ash saw patches of green grass followed by bits of blue sky as the plane tumbled and spun. When it finally came to rest, Ash was upside down in the cockpit. He managed to undo the straps that held him in his seat and climb out of the plane, scrambling away from the burning wreckage. The plane was destroyed, but he, somehow, was alive with just a few scratches.

But for how long? he wondered. He saw a German plane flying low overhead and knew it was looking for him. Ash hid in some bushes, his chest tightening as the plane circled above him. If the German pilot had spotted him, Ash knew a truckload of Germans would soon be rushing to his hiding spot. He watched the plane finally head off, then he scanned the roads. He saw nothing. He felt safe—for now.

Ash crawled out from under the bushes and began walking down a nearby road. It led to a tiny village. Ash knew he had landed not too far from the English Channel, the body of water between France and England. He hoped he could reach the coast and find a way to get across the channel and back to England.

Ash approached a small cottage just off the road. The front door opened, and a young woman grabbed him by the arm and pulled him inside. Ash thought she had a kind face, though it seemed a little sad. He imagined that she had seen more than her share of the horrors of the war already. He began to speak quickly. "Ma'am, I'm a pilot with the RAF, and—"

She motioned for him to stop talking. She didn't seem to speak English, but she seemed to understand his situation. The woman opened a closet and pointed to some men's clothes. Ash nodded. He realized that he couldn't go walking around the French countryside dressed as an RAF pilot. The Nazis had already defeated France and had

troops all over the country. He was sure that word of his crash had spread quickly and that German troops would now be looking for him. Ash quickly changed into the civilian clothes, thanked the woman, and headed out.

After three days of wandering with almost no food, Ash came to a village called Quercamps. Struggling to find the energy to keep moving, he stumbled down the main street. Passing a closed restaurant, he heard voices coming from inside. The voices stopped when Ash knocked on the door.

The door opened a crack. Ash knew just enough French to explain what had happened. The owner of the restaurant, an elderly man named Boulanger, looked Ash up and down. The Frenchman turned to the others with him in the restaurant. They spoke quickly and quietly in French. Finally, Boulanger faced Ash again and motioned for him to come in.

Boulanger led Ash to the kitchen at the back of the restaurant. The sight and smell of food made his stomach grumble. Ash realized he hadn't eaten a real meal since before he had left England days earlier. Mrs. Boulanger saw how he was eyeing the food. With a smile, she began to make him a large plate of eggs. With each bite, Ash thought it was the best food he had ever tasted.

After the meal, the Boulangers took Ash to a small room in the back of the cellar. Mrs. Boulanger pointed to a bed where he could sleep. In the cellar, Ash met the Boulangers' children: Marthe, a teenager, and her younger brother, Julien. That night, Ash slept deeper and longer than he ever had before. For the moment, at least, he felt safe.

◆◆◆

Over the next few days, Ash continued to eat and sleep, slowly regaining his strength. He sometimes joined the Boulangers in the restaurant, but most of the time he stayed hidden in the cellar. No one knew when German soldiers might come to the restaurant.

For several weeks, the Boulangers fed Ash and let him stay in their cellar. One night, as he slept, Ash was startled awake. He saw the two Boulanger children standing above him.

"It's the Germans," Marthe, the oldest, whispered. "They are coming to search the village." Her younger brother, Julien, then said with a shaky voice, "You must go. They will search our cellar, for sure."

Ash nodded and dressed quickly, then followed the two children out of the house and into the fields. They led him to the house of Emile Rocourt. "He is a very important man in the region," Marthe explained. "The Germans won't bother him."

Ash soon saw the Rocourts' large home on the edge of the village. Mr. Rocourt greeted him at the door and led Ash to an old mill on his land.

"The Germans won't come here?" Ash asked, wanting to make sure that Marthe was right.

"They sometimes come to the house," Mr. Rocourt said. "But I will tell them everything is fine and there have been no strangers around. They'll believe me. You'll be safe here."

Ash went into the mill. He tried to be as calm as Mr. Rocourt was. It wasn't easy, knowing both of them would end up in jail if the Germans found him. Through a window, Ash saw German vehicles speeding through the village streets. He held his breath when one truck filled with soldiers slowed down as it neared the Rocourts' driveway. *Please, just keep going*, Ash thought. He let out a deep breath as the German truck rolled past the driveway. A few hours later, Marthe came back for him; the Germans had left the village.

Back at the Boulangers', Ash once again spent most of his time in the cellar, until the Germans returned for another inspection. Again, he headed to the Rocourts' for safety. One day in the

Boulangers' kitchen, Ash finally spoke up.

"You have all done so much for me. I can never repay you. But I'm healthy now, and I need to get back to England, so I can fight again."

"We were glad to help," Mr. Boulanger said. "I wish we could do more."

"We can," Marthe said. "I can take him to the Resistance."

Ash had learned all about the Resistance during his training in England. It was made up of French civilians secretly working against the Germans who now controlled their country. Ash and other RAF pilots knew the Resistance would help them if their planes crashed in France. Members of the Resistance could be able to get him back to England.

Marthe contacted Mr. Rocourt, who soon put Ash in touch with a local Resistance member named Jean. As the two men shook hands, Jean said, "It will be dangerous, of course, to get you out of France. But I think we can do it."

"When?" Ash asked.

"Right now."

◆◆◆

THE RESISTANCE TO GERMAN RULE

Even before the start of World War II, Nazi Germany began seizing control of other nations across Europe. The German control of these nations was called an "occupation." To fight these occupations, some people in the defeated countries tried to find ways to resist German rule.

This resistance could take many forms. Some people printed newspapers that shared the facts of what was happening during the war, since newspapers under German control only printed what the Nazis told them to.

In occupied Denmark, even teens did their part. They printed posters that called on Danes to destroy machinery used to make goods that the Germans needed. Some went so far as to steal rifles from a German barracks. Other Danes protected Jewish citizens when the Germans wanted to send them to the death camps.

Sometimes US and British secret agents parachuted into occupied countries to bring Resistance groups resources like radios and weapons. At times, the agents and the Resistance members blew up railroads and bridges that the Germans needed to move their troops and supplies in occupied lands.

The Resistance was particularly useful in France, as Bill Ash learned. Members helped pilots shot down by German planes. Some took more direct action and killed German military officers. As in other countries, teens and women played important roles in the French Resistance. They often carried messages from one Resistance group to another, and some women smuggled weapons as well.

After the war ended, Bill Ash returned to France to learn what had happened to the people who had helped him before his capture. The woman whose cottage he had first approached was named Pauline Le Cam. She heard Ash's plane crash and was prepared to help him. She was later arrested by the Nazis, who forced her to work for them in a factory.

Marthe Boulanger, the teenage daughter of the French family that took Ash in, went on to work closely with the Resistance. The Germans finally caught her and sent her to a concentration camp, but she survived the war. Both she and Le Cam received a medal from the French government for their service. The man who traveled with Ash after he left the Boulangers', Ash learned, was named Jean de la Olla. He was also arrested, then tortured, but he too survived the war.

After a quick meal, Ash and Jean began their journey to Paris. From there, the Resistance would try to get Ash to Spain, which was not involved in the war. He couldn't risk trying to travel directly to England, since the Germans controlled the ports and airports. After reaching Spain by train, he could safely sail to England.

As he traveled with Jean, Ash had to fight back nerves. German troops patrolled train stations and city streets, and they seemed to stare at him with menacing looks. He felt like they could tell he was not a simple French farmer. But Jean got him safely to Paris. There, he shared an apartment with two other Resistance members.

"We cannot get you to Spain right away," Jean explained. "The Germans have captured some of our members who were going to help you. But we will be ready to get you out soon."

Ash enjoyed his stay in Paris. Even though German troops filled the city, he no longer felt afraid. He carried false papers that said he was a French citizen. And in such a large city, he did not stick out. But his Paris "vacation" soon came to an end.

On a June night, as Ash and the two Resistance members slept, a loud banging jolted Ash awake. He realized that someone with heavy boots was kicking at the apartment door. In seconds, several armed Germans burst in and dragged Ash and the others out of bed.

With guns pointing at him, Ash tried to protect the two Resistance members.

"They don't know me," he said. "We just met. Don't hurt—"

"Shut up," the German said. Ash felt the butt end of a rifle crack into his face. Pain shot up his cheek and into his head.

He must be from the Gestapo, Ash thought. He knew that the Gestapo were the most brutal of all the troops and police that worked for Hitler. The men dragged Ash out the door and drove him to Gestapo headquarters. There, in a small room, Ash tried to explain again that his two roommates were innocent. Then he added, "I'm a Royal Canadian Airforce pilot, and I expect to be treated as a prisoner of war."

"But perhaps you are actually a spy," the Gestapo officer said. "And we don't put spies in prison. We kill them."

THE POWS OF WORLD WAR II

Bill Ash was one of many thousands of Americans who spent time in German prisoner-of-war camps. Germany built hundreds of camps in its own country and in the countries it defeated during the war. One of the largest German camps held about ninety-three thousand prisoners from various countries. Over the course of the war, the Germans captured almost six million Soviet prisoners. Stalag Luft III, where Ash spent much of his time as a prisoner, held as many as eleven thousand prisoners at a time.

Germany managed its prisoners according to a series of international agreements called the Geneva Conventions, named for the city in Switzerland where they were developed. These agreements spelled out how prisoners of war should be treated: POWs were entitled to receive Red Cross packages full of useful items, and had the chance to do such things as play sports, take classes, and stage plays. Prisoners could also send and receive mail and packages from home.

Not all countries treated their prisoners of war the same. The Japanese, for example, forced most prisoners to work. They built railroads and bridges in the lands Japan conquered, and some were sent to Japan to work in coal mines and factories. About 20 percent of the prisoners died because of the harsh treatment they received.

Americans also kept prisoners during the war, and about four hundred thousand captured German troops were sent to camps across the United

States. Many of the prisoners worked on farms. Under the rules of the Geneva Conventions, they were paid for this work. Most of the prisoners were treated well, and US officials hoped that treatment would encourage Germany to do the same with Americans held in German POW camps.

The Gestapo officer wanted to know the names of everyone who had helped Ash since he was shot down. Ash thought about Marthe, the teen who had helped him hide and connected him to the Resistance. He thought about Jean, who had saved him from discovery in the countryside by bringing him to Paris, where he could hide and blend in. He thought, *I can't betray the people who helped save my life.* He refused to reveal the names.

The officer called in two men. One took Ash by the arms, and the other began to pummel his face. Blood flowed from the cuts on his face, and Ash was sure he was going to pass out. Finally, the beating stopped.

"Tell me the names," the officer demanded.

"No," Ash said again. "I'm a pilot and prisoner of war. I don't have to tell you anything."

"Prove you are a pilot," the officer said, "or you will be shot tomorrow."

The officer motioned for the two men to take Ash away.

The next morning, two guards came to drag Ash out of his cell. But instead of taking him to a firing squad, they took him back to the Gestapo officer.

"Are you ready to talk now?" he asked.

"Never," Ash said.

The beating began again—more bruises, more bleeding. Then the guards took him back to the cell. This pattern went on for several days—more questions, no answers, more beatings. Then, a new officer came to Ash's cell. He was in the Luftwaffe, the German air force. Two soldiers stood at the officer's side.

"Come with me," the officer said. "We have determined you are a prisoner of war and the Gestapo has no right to hold you."

Ash was too weak to walk by himself, so the soldiers helped him. Soon, he was on a train to a German POW camp. *I don't know what I'll find there*, he thought. *But it can't be any worse than this.*

Chapter Four

THE URGE TO ESCAPE

After taking the train to Germany, Ash got on a truck that took him to Dulag Luft, an interrogation camp near Frankfurt, Germany. All captured Allied air force pilots and crew were taken there once they reached Germany, before being sent on to other prison camps. It was now early June—more than two months since Ash crashed in France.

Ash faced more questioning at Dulag Luft, but at least this time nobody beat him. And here, he could talk with other captured pilots. Some of the officers helped the newcomers adjust to life as prisoners. But Ash didn't want to adjust. He wanted to escape and fly again.

Not long after arriving at the POW camp Ash met Paddy Barthropp. He was as eager to escape as Ash was. Together, they learned the routines of prison life. They shared cramped rooms with other prisoners in four wooden buildings called barracks. Through the window, they could see farms and a river, and most of the guards treated them well. The Germans hoped that this treatment might make the prisoners willing to share information the Nazis would find useful. Ash, though, did not offer any information.

The prisoners went out several times a day for roll call, entering a large open area surrounded by a barbed-wire fence. Each day, they ate lousy food. One common meal was some kind of fish that smelled like wet dog hair. Somehow, Ash forced it down.

A rare bright spot in POW life was the arrival of packages from the Red Cross, although the prisoners never knew when they might show up. Ash looked forward to the chocolate, canned meat, and other food he usually found inside the package.

After a short stay at Dulag Luft, the Germans herded Ash, Barthropp, and other prisoners into a truck and drove them to Stalag Luft III. Waiting when they got there was the camp commandant, Colonel Friedrich Wilhelm Von Lindeiner. The prisoners stood in rows as the colonel walked up and down past them. "For you, the war is over," the colonel said. "But we will try to make your stay a pleasant one. That way, you will have no reason to try to escape. For as you will discover, escaping is impossible."

Ash leaned over to Barthropp and whispered, "There's always a first time."

It didn't take long for Ash to meet the men at the camp who were most eager to escape. One of them was Douglas Bader. Like most RAF pilots, Ash knew all about him. Bader had lost both his legs in a plane crash before the war. The RAF said he would never fly for it again.

But using artificial legs, Bader did fly when World War II began, and he was one of Britain's best fighter pilots. At Stalag Luft III, Ash was inspired by Bader's desire to continue fighting the

Germans in whatever ways possible. He encouraged other prisoners to rebel too.

One day soon after Ash arrived, the entire camp was called out for a roll call.

"What's going on?" Ash asked Bader.

"Some chaps tried to escape last night," Bader said. "Now the goons are trying to figure out how many got out. But I think we can throw them off a bit."

Bader told Ash, Barthropp, and some other men who had not yet been counted to mix in with the prisoners who had been counted.

"My pleasure!" Ash said, eager to follow Bader's order. Letting out a whoop, Ash led the men across the camp. But his excitement quickly faded as a couple of guards grabbed him and Barthropp and led them at gunpoint outside the camp.

After tramping a few hundred feet, the guards ordered them to stop and forced them to their knees. The soldiers stood behind them, and Ash could picture a rifle pointing at his head. *Go ahead*, he thought, *if you're going to kill me, kill me*. Seconds passed, but the soldiers did not fire.

Instead, they brought Ash and Barthropp back to the camp, where each was given two weeks in what the prisoners called "the cooler," a concrete cell where a prisoner would be held alone, in solitary confinement. *They just wanted to scare us*, Ash thought. *Well, it didn't work.*

The guards led Barthropp to one cooler and Ash to another. Ash looked around the tiny cell, just ten feet long and four feet wide, with only one small barred window high above the floor. It had a bed, a table, and a stool. For the first few days, Ash had only bread and water to eat and drink. The Germans would not let him bring in a book, so he tried to remember poems and stories he had read in school.

At times, he jumped up and grabbed the bars on the tiny window. He thought, *I just need a quick look at the world outside this place.* Each night, a guard came and took away his shoes. "So you can't escape," the guard said with a laugh. He knew, just as Ash did, that there was no way out of the cooler.

As his days in the cooler passed, the Germans

gave him a little more food, but hunger still burned in his stomach. He missed talking to the other men. Finally, after two weeks, his time in the cooler ended. Ash and Barthropp rejoined the other prisoners. They saw Bader, who smiled.

"You two did all right," he said. "Make sure you keep making things hard for the goons."

"What about you?" Ash asked.

"Colonel Von Lindeiner has had enough of me," Bader said, smiling again. "They're sending me to another camp."

Many of the prisoners came out to watch as forty soldiers led Bader out of the camp on his artificial legs. With Bader gone, Ash was more determined than ever to escape. He remembered what Bader had once said: "We might not be able to fly anymore, but we can still fight." Trying to escape was part of that fight.

Soon, Ash and Barthropp came up with their plan to hide out in the space beneath the showers before making their break for freedom.

Most escape attempts relied on digging tunnels, but the ferrets had already found some shallow ones at the camp. Digging a much deeper tunnel would take months and plenty of men. Ash didn't want to wait that long.

He and Barthropp went to see the officers that formed the escape committee, and Ash described his plan to hide out in the shower building and make a break from there. When he finished, committee leader Jimmy Buckley told them to wait outside the barracks. A few minutes later, Buckley called them back inside.

"We like it," he said. "We'll do everything we can to make it work."

But as Ash and Barthropp later learned, every plan has its risks. When the guards found him hiding under the showers, Ash remembered how sure he had been that he could escape. He went to the cooler for the second time, where he had plenty of opportunity to think about escaping again. When he got out two weeks later, a guard was waiting for him. He told Ash to join a group of about ninety prisoners in the center of the camp.

"What's happening?" Ash asked Jimmy Buckley.

"You're on the 'list.' Barthropp too. They're

sending us to a camp in Poland. They say it's getting too crowded here."

But Ash couldn't help but notice that many of the men going to Poland were the same men intent on escaping. Maybe the Germans thought the new camp would crush their desire. Ash thought, *These Nazis just don't understand us. We'll try again—wherever they put us.*

Chapter Five

ANOTHER TRY

For thirty-six hours, Bill Ash and the other prisoners being transferred sat on stiff wooden seats
on the train they were riding toward their new
camp in Schubin, Poland. When they arrived, they
immediately saw something that they believed
would help with an escape. The camp had been
built as a school, not a prison, and some of the
buildings were close to the barbed-wire fences
that surrounded the place.

"This means we don't have to dig long tunnels,"
Ash noted.

"And if we do get out," Barthropp said, "we'll
be in a country that hates the Germans as much
as we do."

Back in the United States, Ash had read plenty of newspaper reports about Germany's brutal invasion of Poland in 1939. More than one hundred thousand Poles had died or been sent to prison since Germany's invasion. Because of that, Ash figured he could count on the help of many Polish civilians, even though they risked being shot by the German forces in their country. Of course, Ash knew he had to get out of the prison camp first.

Once the new prisoners settled in, members of the new camp's escape committee asked Ash and Barthropp to join them. Ash liked the idea that now he would have a say in how escapes would be carried out. But before the committee approved a major escape attempt, Ash decided to try one on his own.

The camp held both officers and men of lower rank. By international law, the officers did not have to work. But Ash decided to join a group of privates who were being sent out of the camp to unload supplies at the local train station. A long coat covered his lieutenant's uniform, but one of the privates recognized him as an officer.

"What are *you* doing?" the private asked.

Ash replied with a smile, "Oh, I just thought I'd get some fresh air outside the camp."

As the prisoners marched to the station, German soldiers kept their rifles ready. At the station, Ash kept an eye on the guards as he approached a train. When the guards weren't looking, he slipped between the train cars and ducked behind the train on the opposite side of the tracks. He scanned the countryside. Surrounding the station was a large, open field, but beyond that was the edge of a forest. *If I can just reach those trees*, Ash thought, *I might have a chance.*

Ash took a deep breath, then sprinted away from the train. In seconds, he heard a rifle shot ring out and felt a bullet whiz over his head. He was still far away from the forest. As he ran, Ash looked back and saw two German soldiers on bicycles quickly gaining on him. They soon circled around him.

I guess I should give up, Ash thought. But the idea flashed out of his head, and instead he tried

to plow through the two men. A rifle butt smashed into his face, and Ash crumpled to the ground. His head throbbing with pain, Ash knew he was due for another trip to the cooler.

Weeks later, as winter approached, Ash came up with another escape idea. He gathered with a group of men outside the latrine, the building that held the prisoners' toilets.

"We should start a tunnel here," he said. "Inside the latrine, the goons won't see us digging, and we have a reason to be in there anytime. Plus, it's only about 150 feet to the outside of the camp." The other men liked the idea. Soon, about twenty-four prisoners were at work digging their tunnel.

Inside the latrine, the men removed some of the concrete bricks in one wall and began to dig. The latrine had a large pit to collect human waste. The awful smell from the pit filled their noses, but the men tried to ignore it. And Ash knew the pit was actually a good thing. Once a month, Polish civilians came to pump out the waste—and any dirt that was mixed into it.

"The pit is perfect for us," Ash said. "We can hide the dirt we dig in there." That solved one of the biggest problems in digging an escape tunnel—where to hide the dirt so the guards wouldn't see it. Another challenge was keeping the camp's ferrets from hearing the digging. The Germans put microphones underground to listen for the sounds diggers would make. Ash and the others decided to dig their tunnel almost twenty feet below the surface, to make it harder for the microphones to pick up the sound.

Ash and a Canadian prisoner named Eddy Asselin were in charge of the digging. Paddy Barthropp and several others helped out, and eventually all twenty-four men took turns shoveling out the dirt. While that work went on, other men tried to get useful information and items. They were called "traders," and they talked to friendly guards or Polish civilians who worked in the camp. The men traded cigarettes and chocolate from their Red Cross packages for maps and other practical things, such as clothing. Prisoners who were called "tailors" used that clothing and some sent by the Red Cross to make clothes similar to what the locals had for the escapees to wear when they left the camp.

In the tunnel, the work was slow and steady. Since they were working in almost total darkness, Ash and the others carried small lamps made from tin cans filled with margarine, which would burn, and a shoelace as a wick.

To make it easier to breathe in the tight space, the men fashioned a long tube made of empty metal cans. The cans had come in their Red Cross packages. The POWs turned a canvas bag into a bellows—a device for pumping air. Someone outside the tunnel moved the bellows back and forth to pump fresh air through the cans down to the men digging below.

To keep the tunnel from collapsing, the men took wooden boards from their beds and used them to brace the dirt walls and ceiling. Ash soon had no boards left on his bed, and he slept on top of a net he made from string, which held up his mattress.

As the tunnel grew longer, some of the men

began to worry a bit. "It's so cramped in there," Asselin said to Ash. "Even with the air pumps, sometimes I feel like I can't breathe. And what if the tunnel collapses?"

"Then we die," Ash said calmly. "Come on, we've gone sixty feet already. Keep digging."

Ash tried to encourage the others, but he knew that this was no easy task. At times, the margarine lamps went out, and the men worked in total darkness. The cold clay and dirt that surrounded them seemed to fill their bodies, and bits of earth sometimes fell all around them. To make it worse, smells from the latrine sometimes filled the tunnel, making the men gag.

In the worst moments, Ash thought to himself, *all this will be worth it when we finally get out.* And when the thought of quitting flashed through his head, he remembered his plane crash. He pictured Marthe and Julien Boulanger and all the brave Resistance members who had risked their lives to help him. He thought of the people across Europe suffering because of the Nazis. Then he took his little tin scoop and went back to chipping away again at the dirt wall in front of him.

The digging and the planning for the escape took months. Finally, in March 1943, one year after he crash-landed and about six months after arriving at Schubin, the tunnel was ready. On March 5, a moonless night, thirty-three men prepared to go. They wore clothing made by the tailors. They carried forged papers that said they were civilians. These papers even had photographs. A friendly Polish worker had sneaked a camera to the prisoners for that purpose. After the five p.m. roll call, the men began to head to the latrine. They waited for several hours before starting to crawl through the tunnel. Ash felt as he had before taking off in his Spitfire—a little nervous, but totally excited.

Ash and Asselin were the first in line to go through the tunnel. They had the job of digging out the last bit of dirt on the surface outside the camp. As they waited for the signal to go, they discussed their plans. "We'll head for Warsaw," Ash said. Asselin nodded. In the Polish capital, they could contact the Resistance there. Some of the men were going to try to take trains, but Ash preferred to go on foot. "The Poles will help us, I know," he said. "Look at how many have already risked their lives so we could get this far with the tunnel."

As the men gathered in the latrine, Ash explained to some who had not been in the tunnel before what it would be like. "You have to push your bag in front of you as you crawl on your knees. Use your elbows and toes, too. Whatever you do, don't grab at the wooden boards! If one comes down, the whole tunnel could collapse."

By seven thirty p.m., twenty-six men were on their knees inside the tunnel. The rest waited in the latrine for their turn. Asselin and Ash dug out the last bit of earth at the end of the tunnel. Asselin broke through the ground first. Soon, Ash saw trees and bushes above him and felt the cold night air. He took a deep breath, smiled, and then turned to his partner.

"Eddy, that's what freedom smells like."

ON THE RUN

Ash and Asselin kept digging, tearing through dirt and the roots of plants. When they popped their heads up, they saw that the tunnel had gone exactly where it was supposed to—into a potato field beyond the wire fence. Asselin started to speak, but Ash put his hand over his friend's mouth and gestured toward the camp. A soldier was on patrol just inside the fence. Asselin's eyes widened as he followed Ash's movement and spotted the guard himself. He nodded to Ash, who slowly removed his hand from his friend's mouth. The guard, meanwhile, came closer to the fence. But he kept his eyes focused on the camp. He walked by without glancing toward the potato field.

The pair began to crawl along the dirt, taking cover in ditches that ran through the field. Then, they got up and made a run for the nearby forest. Hearing his footsteps hit twigs, Ash thought, *It's so loud—I'm so loud!* But he realized that was just his fear of being discovered so soon after leaving the tunnel. Back inside the camp's fence, none of the guards heard a thing.

At the edge of the forest, Ash and Asselin stopped.

"You're okay?" Ash whispered. Asselin nodded. "Then let's go!"

They started running again. Ash listened for the sound of rifle shots or shrieking alarms, which would mean the Nazis had seen them or the others now scrambling out of the tunnel. But the night remained silent. *I'm free*, Ash thought. *I'm finally free.* All those weeks of digging out the dark, cramped tunnel had paid off.

The two POWs moved as fast as they could, though in spots the wet ground slowed them down. They avoided roads and houses as much

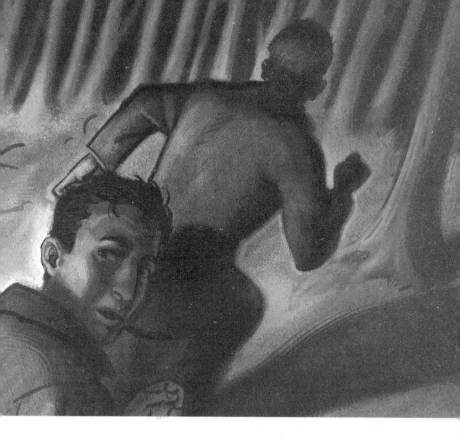

as possible, so they wouldn't be spotted. Finally, just before sunrise, they collapsed under a group of tall trees.

"How far do you think we got?" Asselin asked.

"At least ten miles. Maybe more."

As they settled onto the ground to sleep, Ash thought about all he had been through. In the past year he had been beaten, locked in the cooler, and gone hungry. But he never lost his will to be free and to fight again. He was proud of all he had done. But he knew that when daylight came, the Nazis would discover the escape. Hundreds, maybe thousands, of Germans would begin searching the countryside, looking for him and the others. He tried not to think about that as he fell asleep on a bed of dry leaves.

When they woke, Ash and Asselin spent the rest of the day hiding in the same spot. That night, they heard German soldiers nearby, the beams of their flashlights cutting through the darkness. Ash sat motionless as the searchers passed within just a few feet of where he and Asselin hid. Somehow, the Germans didn't see them.

For almost a week, Ash and Asselin kept moving toward Warsaw. They ate the Mixture they had brought, then searched for vegetables stored at farms. For water, they drank from streams. When they could, they slept in barns. One night, they came to a bridge guarded by a soldier at each end.

"We should keep going," Asselin said. "We can cross the river farther down."

"It's too deep to wade across," Ash said. "And

we'd be out in the open, where they could see us. Let's take a chance here."

Each German soldier had a small shelter he could use to find some warmth on cold nights. Ash and Asselin waited for the guards to enter their shelters, then slowly made their way, crawling across the bridge. Shadows helped hide them, but at one point, one of the guards left his shelter and approached the bridge. The escapees froze. But the guard stopped and turned back without seeing them. Ash and Asselin continued their crawl. They reached the other side of the river and headed for the woods. Ash let out a deep breath.

"That was close. I hope this trip gets a little easier from this point on."

By then, several days had passed since the escape. Everyone in the region knew that thirty-three prisoners had gotten out of the POW camp. And Ash soon learned that not all the local people were against the Nazis. One chilly morning, he and Asselin woke up and saw that they were surrounded by farmers with pitchforks.

"Should we run?" Asselin whispered.

"I don't think we'd have a chance," Ash said. "Look over there." He pointed past the small group of farmers. A woman was coming toward them with several German soldiers right behind her. When she and the soldiers reached Ash and Asselin, she began pointing and shouting in German.

"Do you know what she's saying?" Ash asked.

"I think she wants them to shoot us."

The soldiers approached Ash and Asselin and ordered them to stand. Then they marched them to the nearest village and threw them in jail. Ash glanced at Asselin, who looked like a beaten man.

"This is it for me," he told Ash. "No more escapes. I feel like if I try again, I'll end up dead."

"I know it," Ash said. "It's dangerous."

"So what will happen now?"

"The soldiers here will take us back to the camp in Schubin," Ash explained. "You, me, and anyone else they've rounded up will spend some time in the cooler. And then some of us will try to figure out another way to escape."

The next morning, just as Ash had predicted, the captured prisoners were driven back to the camp and each was tossed into his own cooler cell. Ash soon learned that most of the men had been recaptured. One had gotten more than five hundred miles by train before the Germans found him.

When he got out of the cooler, Ash learned how well the escape had gone—at first. The guards had not discovered that the men were missing until after eight a.m. on the morning of March 6, about ten hours after Ash and Asselin had first popped out of the tunnel. The guards searched the entire camp looking for Ash and the others.

Ash also learned that the camp commandant had been punished and replaced for failing to prevent the escape. The new commandant and his team were determined to stop future attempts. But Ash soon learned that his next escape attempt would not be made at Schubin. In April, he and the other recaptured prisoners boarded trucks and headed back to Stalag Luft III.

Chapter Seven

ANOTHER CAMP, ANOTHER ESCAPE

Pulling into the camp, Ash could see that the Germans had expanded Stalag Luft III over the past few months. Some of the new buildings housed captured US pilots. The Americans had been flying missions in Europe since the summer of 1942, seven months after the United States finally entered the war.

"It's nice to see so many Americans again," Ash said to Asselin. But he soon realized that he wouldn't have much contact with his fellow countrymen. The RAF pilots and the Americans were kept in separate compounds. Barbed-wire fences cut off one from the other, and guards with machine guns watched the strip of dirt that stood between them. The POWs called it "no-man's-land."

Ash learned that some of his old friends at Stalag Luft III were still trying to dig tunnels, and that new men had joined them. But the effort had gotten much harder.

"The ferrets have gotten smarter," one British officer told him. "They drive heavy vehicles around the camp, hoping to make tunnels collapse. And they measure the dirt under the barracks. When it starts going up, they know we're putting there what we've dug out."

"I wonder if it would be easier to get out of another camp," Ash said.

"Maybe. But you're in this one."

Ash smiled. "For now."

He was already working on a new escape plan. He had heard that a group of sergeants were going to be moved from Stalag Luft III to a camp in Lithuania. *If I can get in with those guys*, Ash thought, *I can get to that other camp—one that might be easier to break out of.* Officers like Ash lived in different compounds from the sergeants who were

going to be moved, with a barbed-wire fence in between them. Keeping a careful eye out for the guards, Ash was able to speak with prisoners on the other side of the fence. Communicating this way, Ash found a New Zealand sergeant named Don Fair who was ready to change places with him. Fair did not want to try an escape himself, but he was willing to help out a fellow prisoner. Plus, if he pretended to be an officer, Fair would no longer risk being sent to Lithuania.

"All we have to do is swap identity papers," Ash said. "You'll become Bill Ash, and I'll be Don Fair."

Fair looked doubtful. "Except first we have to get out of our fenced-in areas without the guards killing us."

Ash recruited some other officers to pretend to start a fight. Their shouts distracted the guards. Then Ash and Fair each carefully scrambled up the wire fence that surrounded their compounds. They met in the no-man's-land in between. Ash stuck out his hand to shake Fair's, and then the two men traded papers.

"Good luck, Sergeant Fair," the real Fair said to Ash with a smile.

Ash then began to climb up the other wire fence. It was ten feet tall, but as he went up, Ash felt like it was one hundred feet. He waited for a rifle shot and the piercing pain of a bullet hitting him in the back. It never came. The guards were watching the fake fight and didn't spot him. Ash dropped down safely into the other compound. Soon, he and the others headed to the train station for the trip to their new "home."

It didn't take long for the prisoners at the new camp, Stalag Luft VI, to learn who "Sergeant Don Fair" really was and to hear about his vast experience with trying to escape POW camps. Ash was soon on this camp's escape committee. The committee went to work creating an organized system for planning and carrying out escapes. Part of the system included finding traders to get the important supplies they would need. Another part was focusing on one tunnel at a time.

Ash and some other prisoners began digging a tunnel under a laundry room. But unlike in Schubin, the men could not dig too deep. If they did, water from underground springs would rush into the tunnel. At the same time, the tunnel could not be too close to the surface. Once again, the ferrets had microphones to listen for the sound of digging.

The work was slow and steady, as the tunnel grew to 150 feet long. The leader of the prisoners in the compound, Jimmy Deans, congratulated Ash on their progress.

"But I think the commandant knows something is going on," Deans said. "He asked if I knew anything about a tunnel."

"What did you say?" Ash asked.

"I said I didn't know of anything going on in the camp that shouldn't be going on." Deans then added with a smile, "Of course, in my opinion, digging a tunnel is exactly what should be going on in a POW camp."

The commandant, however, remained suspicious. Soon, Gestapo men were crawling through the camp, looking for signs of an escape attempt. Ash saw them carry maps and clothing out of several barracks. *But no sign that they found the tunnel*, Ash thought to himself. Still, the escape committee knew the Germans were focused on finding their tunnel, if it existed. The diggers had brought the tunnel outside the camp, but they were short of the planned target, which was a group of trees that would help hide the escape. The men discussed what to do next.

"Keep digging," someone said. "We've kept the tunnel a secret for this long."

Ash shook his head. "I say stop digging and get as many men out now, while we can. The more we dig, the more we risk the Nazis finding it."

Finally, the men who were to take part in the escape voted. They wanted to stop digging and get out as soon as they could.

On the night of the escape, fifty men prepared to go. In their beds, they left behind dummies made from papier-mâché, with their heads covered with real hair. The men had made the dummies in art classes the Germans offered, part of their efforts as spelled out in the Geneva Conventions to help the prisoners pass the time.

As in Schubin, Ash was at the front of the line in the tunnel. Though he had favored the early escape, he worried about what he would find on the surface. *The tunnel comes out close to the fence*, he thought. *And those trees are a long way out.*

He pushed through the long, dark tunnel. The men had set up a system to bring in fresh air while they were digging, but it was no longer working. The farther Ash went, the more he struggled to breathe. Finally, he reached the spot where the tunnel turned upward, toward the surface. He dug out the last bit of dirt and felt cool, fresh air wash over him. He took a deep breath. "Oh, that is good," he said to himself. Behind him, he heard the others sigh with relief as the air began to reach them.

Ash poked his head above the ground. He heard footsteps nearby, inside the camp, and ducked back down. When the German guard passed, he climbed out of the hole. Bracing himself, he dashed toward the trees about thirty feet away. *Thirty feet*, he thought. *Might as well be thirty miles when you know you might take a bullet any second.*

Ash made it to the trees, then looked back to see other men popping out of the tunnel and sprinting toward him. But he didn't watch for long. He turned and started running through the trees. He hadn't gotten far when he heard gunfire behind him. *The Nazis have spotted us*, he thought. The rifle shots were quickly followed by the barks of the Germans' dogs. Ash put his head down and ran as fast as he could.

Chapter Eight

A TRIP TO BERLIN

As he ran, Ash looked back and saw searchlights from the camp scanning the countryside. Sirens blared as more gunshots rang out. *Faster*, Ash thought to himself, *run faster!* He heard the German dogs barking as they raced through the woods.

Ash came to a small river and jumped in. *If I can get to the other side, the dogs will lose my scent in the water.* His whole body shivered as he swam across the freezing-cold river. When he reached the other side, he could hear the dogs barking as they searched for his scent. But Ash quickly realized that the dogs and their Nazi handlers had turned away from the river. He was safe—for now.

Even though the Germans had turned back, Ash kept running. He passed through swampy lands surrounded by tall trees. Their leaves seemed to glow in the faint light of the approaching dawn. He'd been running for almost six hours now. He stopped to rest, but not for long. The Germans would not rest in their search for him and the others who had managed to escape.

Ash kept moving for several days, using a small compass to help guide him. He headed east toward the Soviet Union. The Nazis had invaded that country earlier in the war, but now Soviet forces were driving them back toward Germany. Most of the Soviet troops came from Russia. *If I'm lucky*, Ash thought, *I'll meet up with some Russians before the Germans find me.*

With each passing day, Ash felt himself get weaker, having spent so much energy the weeks before, digging the tunnel. And even on the best days, the meals the Germans had served left him hungry. Now, he ate only tiny bits of the Mixture, trying to make it last.

On one moonlit night, he found a small building on the edge of a farm. Slipping inside, he curled up in a pile of straw and tried to sleep. During the time he had been on the run, he hadn't slept well. The smallest noise from a nearby animal or a creaking tree was enough to make him jump awake. This time, as morning came, it was the touch of cold steel against his skin that prodded him from his sleep.

Ash woke to see a group of Lithuanian farmers standing over him. One held a pitchfork.

It's like being found by those German farmers all over again, Ash thought. The man with the pitchfork asked if he were German or Russian. "I'm from Texas," Ash said, and he could see that none of them had ever heard of the place. But at least the farmers seemed friendly after that. They gave him a pitchfork and motioned for him to work with them in the fields.

For several days, he worked with the Lithuanians. They fed him, and when German troops came by, the farmers acted as if Ash were one of them. But soon Ash decided it was time to move

on. Using sign language and simple German, Ash tried to communicate with the farmers.

"Where can I get a boat so I can go to Sweden?" he asked. Sweden had remained neutral in the war. If he made it there, he could get back to England. The men pointed and tried to draw a map in the dirt. Ash understood—if he headed northwest, he would reach the Baltic Sea. From there, he could sail west for about two hundred miles and reach Sweden. He thanked the farmers and headed out again.

Traveling mostly at night, Ash reached the coast in just a few days. Peering through a window, he saw several boats locked inside a boathouse. He broke the lock to the building and picked out a small sailboat. The only problem was getting it from the boathouse to the sea. Ash tried to drag the boat out of the house. It wouldn't budge. "It would take five guys to haul this thing out," he said to himself. "Where am I going to find four more guys?"

Ash knew that all Lithuanians might not be as friendly as the farmers who had helped him.

But he had to take his chances. He saw a group of men working in a field. Instead of making up some story, he told them the truth: He explained in English that he was an RAF pilot trying to get back to England. He saw the men look at each other and then at him.

"Do you understand me?" Ash asked. He repeated what he had said, using the few words of German he knew. One of the men smiled a little. Ash was shocked to hear him say in almost perfect English, "We would love to help you."

Ash smiled. "That's great! I need—"

The man cut him off. "We would love to help, except, we are German soldiers."

Before Ash could even start to run, the Nazis tackled him, dragged him to his feet, and hand-cuffed him. They pushed him into a car and drove to a nearby town. The car stopped in front of a building. *This must be the local Gestapo*, Ash thought. He remembered the beatings in Paris that had left him bloodied and bruised. Inside the building, the Gestapo agents threw him into a cell. *Well, that's good. No beatings—so far.*

Ash sat in the cell for several days, until finally an officer came to let him out. Standing behind the officer were six stern guards, holding rifles across their chests. The guards and the officer marched him to the nearby train station. *Are they taking me back to Stalag Luft III?* he wondered.

As the train rumbled along for hours, the guards sat silently all around Ash. He looked out the window and saw the devastating effects of the war. What had once been houses and barns were just charred wooden shells. Children in rags played near the huge craters left by bombs. Ash thought, *No one here has escaped the horrors of the war.*

He wondered what horrors might be waiting for him wherever he was going. Soon he had the answer. The train reached the edge of a large city. *Berlin*, Ash realized. *But why Berlin?* Inside the main train station of the German capital, a huge poster of Adolf Hitler hung on the wall. Ash felt like Hitler's dark, beady eyes watched his every step.

Outside the station, a long black car waited for him and his guards. Ash sank into the back seat, afraid of what would happen next. *More beatings?* he wondered. *Even worse than before? Or maybe they'll skip the torture and just kill me.* Ash's mind raced as the car sped through the streets of Berlin. It finally stopped at a building Ash guessed was Gestapo headquarters. The guards roughly pushed him out of the car and into the building.

Inside a small office, a Gestapo officer peered at him through thick glasses.

"So, your name is Donald Fair and you are from New Zealand," the man said.

"That's right," Ash said.

"You did not cause any trouble until you reached Lithuania."

Ash shrugged. "I just thought it was time to try to escape."

The man reached for a thick folder on his desk. Ash could see the name written on it—his name . . . his *real* name.

"We know who you really are," the Gestapo man said. "What do you think will happen to you now?"

"Send me back to Stalag Luft III?" Ash asked.

The man shook his head. "That camp is for

prisoners of war. But we don't think you are a pilot shot down in battle."

"No?" Ash tried to fight back a smile. *Then what am I?* he thought to himself. But before he could say another word, the man explained exactly what the Gestapo thought he was doing.

The Nazis believed that the British had sent him to France so that he would be caught. They thought that Ash was then supposed to teach the prisoners he met how to escape from German prison camps.

"It was a very clever plan," the Gestapo officer said. "But now it is over. And since you are not a real prisoner, we can do what we want with you."

"You mean kill me?"

The man smiled. "Oh, you will have a trial first, so you can claim your innocence. But we know what you are. And yes, you will be shot."

Two guards grabbed Ash and dragged him to a cell. No one beat him. *Why bother?* Ash thought. *They know I'll be dead soon enough.*

The next day, a German officer came to Ash's cell. He explained that he would be his lawyer for the trial. Ash, though, could not actually attend his own trial. The officer would ask him questions and then bring the answers to the court.

Ash asked him, "Is there any chance I can prove I'm just a regular POW?"

The officer shook his head. "I'm afraid not. The Gestapo has already decided. In the end, you will be shot."

Ash slumped in his chair. *Well, I've been pretty lucky so far. But I guess my luck's run out.*

The trial dragged on for several weeks. During that time, US and British bombers attacked Berlin. Locked in his basement cell, Ash heard the explosions and felt the building shake when bombs landed nearby. And he soon learned that his luck had not yet run out. The officer who was defending him in court explained.

"All the records for your case were destroyed in a bombing raid. And the bombing is only getting worse. The Gestapo has decided to end your trial."

As 1944 began, Ash found himself on a train. He was going back to Stalag Luft III after all.

Chapter Nine

THE LAST ESCAPE

I feel like I'm coming home, Ash thought as he entered the camp. He saw many familiar faces in the compound. Paddy Barthropp, though, and some of his other old pals were now in a different compound within the camp.

Ash soon learned that many of the men at Stalag Luft III were already at work on three new tunnels. The prisoners nicknamed them Tom, Dick, and Harry. But before Ash could think about any more underground digging, he was thrown into the cooler.

"They should call you the Cooler King," one prisoner said as the guards hauled Ash toward the tiny cell.

"The Cooler King. I kinda like that," Ash said with a smile. But once inside the cooler, he saw, again, that there was nothing kingly about the tiny cell that would be his home for the next two weeks.

When he got out of the cooler, Ash took some time to rebuild his strength. But it didn't take long for him to try once again to escape. Walking around the compound one day, he saw a truck parked near the gate. It sat with its motor running as a guard searched the back of the truck. When the guard was done, he turned and walked away.

This is my chance, Ash thought as he bolted toward the back of the truck. He jumped in without the guard seeing him. The truck began to head out of the camp, but then Ash felt it slow down and finally stop. Ash heard soldiers outside. Seconds later, one of them peered into the back of the truck and saw him. Within minutes, Ash was back in the cooler.

Ash was used to life in this cell. Mostly, he sat and thought about the war, people he knew, what he had gone through. He thought about his mother back in Texas. She had written to him several times since his capture. In one letter, she described how she was baking apple pies for German POWs held in America. He laughed as he remembered her next line: "I hope the German mothers are doing the same thing for you." Ash hadn't tasted an apple pie in years.

Yeah, the war sure has changed my life, he thought. But he had no regrets about wanting to fight Hitler and Nazis. *Good people have to stand up to evil wherever they see it.* Ash knew the war would be over soon, since the Allies were pounding Germany with bombs every day. But he still wanted to escape and fight the Nazis again.

One night in the cell, Ash heard sirens go off in the camp. "Escape!" he said to himself. "Paddy and the boys must be putting those new tunnels to good use."

But when he finally got out of the cooler in April 1944, Ash learned more about what was soon called the Great Escape. Almost eighty men had fled the camp on the night of March 24. Fifty had been recaptured and shot by the Gestapo. That news stunned Ash and the other prisoners. The Germans were cracking down on escapees—perhaps because they sensed the war was coming to a close and they were going to lose.

THE GREAT ESCAPE

Bill Ash was in the cooler when the biggest escape attempt of the war took place. While several officers played key roles in planning the escape, Roger Bushell was the leader. A pilot who had been shot down in 1940, Bushell had tried to escape several times before he organized the construction of the three tunnels nicknamed Tom, Dick, and Harry. Eventually, Bushell and the others put all their efforts into Harry. When the tunnel was finished, it had electric lights, with the power coming from wiring in the barracks. Using stolen materials, the prisoners built a small railway in the tunnel out of wood.

A cart on wheels rode on the tracks, hauling

out dirt. To get the dirt out of the tunnels, prisoners carried it in bags inside their pants, then dumped the dirt around the compound. The men who carried the dirt using the bags were called penguins, because the bags made them waddle like those birds as they walked. Working this way, the penguins spread out more than one hundred tons of sand.

On the night of the escape, two hundred prisoners were supposed to go out the tunnel. Only seventy-six made it outside Stalag Luft III before the Germans discovered the escape. Three—two Norwegians and a Dutchman—managed to avoid capture and win their freedom. Roger Bushell was one of the fifty POWs recaptured and shot by the Germans.

In 1963, the movie *The Great Escape* showed the efforts of the hundreds of men who built Harry and tried to escape from Stalag Luft III.

While the movie was based on actual events, not everything in it was true. The lead character was an American prisoner named Virgil Hilts, who did not exist in real life. He had the nickname of the "Cooler King." Some people have suggested that Hilts was based on Bill Ash. Ash wrote years later that no one connected with making the movie ever told him he was the model for Hilts. In reality, the filmmakers probably based the character on several real-life POWs.

In any event, the Gestapo decided it would take control of Stalag Luft III and the other prison camps. They were bound to be stricter than the Luftwaffe officers had been. But that wouldn't keep Ash from trying to escape again.

He joined several others to form yet another escape committee in their compound. "We should try to work with the Americans in the compound next door," one officer said. The others on the committee agreed, and they picked Ash to climb the fences separating the compounds to go talk with the Americans. They seemed interested in trying another escape. But a new development in the war soon changed their plans.

Back in his own compound, Ash heard shouting

coming from outside his barracks. "They've landed! The Allies have reached France!"

The news came over one of the simple radios the men had built using stolen and smuggled parts. Finally, the Allies had sent troops to France to push the Germans out of the lands they controlled. Bombing raids had destroyed many German factories, but Ash and so many others knew that a land attack was the only way to truly defeat the Germans and end the war. In the weeks that followed, Ash closely followed the news broadcast over the secret radio. He and the other prisoners tracked the Allies' effort to drive the Germans out of France.

Ash saw that even fewer men were ready to risk an escape now. Two had dug a short tunnel, but now they decided not to use it. Ash, though, was ready to try escape again, and he found two more POWs eager to go with him. The other prisoners, however, did not like the idea.

"If you get caught," one said, "the Gestapo might punish *us*."

Those fears led the commanding officer in the compound to cancel the escape attempt. A disappointed Ash realized he would most likely spend the rest of the war as a prisoner.

By the beginning of 1945, the Allies had reached Belgium and were close to Germany's western border. In Eastern Europe, the Russians were also pushing back the Nazis. The bitterly cold winter was easier to take as the prisoners heard Soviet artillery slowly getting closer.

Soon the Gestapo had the men marching out of Stalag Luft III to another camp miles away in Germany. Day after day, Ash and the others trudged through ice and snow. When the water ran out, the men melted snow and gulped down the cold liquid. Around Ash, prisoners and guards alike developed frostbite as the temperature fell below freezing.

As the men passed through small villages, the residents came out to stare. Ash traded some of the cigarettes and chocolate from his Red Cross packages for food. *I should have grabbed more chocolate*, Ash thought, as he saw how eager the Germans were for this treat.

The marching finally ended when the prisoners reached the small town of Spremberg. There, the soldiers crammed them into train cars normally used to carry cattle. The cars stank from the cattle's waste, and the men were jammed into the car so tightly, they could not sit down. Ash still had no idea where the Germans were taking them, or even if they would let the prisoners live. For days, rumors had spread that they would all be shot.

By now, Ash was sick, his skin turning yellow from a liver disease called jaundice. The Germans took him and other sick prisoners off the train and brought them to a military hospital near the Marlag und Milag Nord camp outside Bremen.

After a few weeks, Ash recovered from his illness. By the spring of 1945, however, the war came to the camp. German troops had taken it over, filling it with tanks and artillery. They were convinced the Allies would not attack their own troops. *I wouldn't bet on that*, Ash thought, and sure enough, British artillery shells soon began to explode within the camp. The Germans returned fire.

As the fighting went on through the day, Ash thought about all his escape attempts so far. *Close to a dozen, I bet. Well, why not go for one more?*

Better to die that way than just sitting here waiting for a shell to hit me.

As bullets flew around him and shells exploded inside and outside the camp, Ash paused for a moment. Despite all he had seen and experienced during the war, he felt his knees shake with fear. The trembling got so bad he could barely stand. Then he heard cries for help coming from the hospital. Men too weak to get out of their beds were just lying inside, with no chance to take cover from the shells landing all around the camp. Ash felt his legs regain their strength. *Somebody's got to help those poor guys*, he thought. *And it might as well be me.*

Several other prisoners had the same idea. They joined Ash as he headed into the hospital. Ash went to a bed and saw a prisoner who could barely move. "Come on, buddy," Ash said. "Let's get you out of here." Ash picked up the man and gently lifted him onto his back. As Ash carried him out of the hospital, he heard the man mumble, "Thank you."

Ash realized he could help more prisoners if he could escape and reach the British lines. *If I tell them where most of the prisoners are, they can try to avoid them when they fire.* With a deep breath, Ash bolted toward the wire fence. One way or another, he knew this would be his last escape.

Bullets whizzed close by as he ran. He dodged the holes in the ground that the exploding shells made, each blast sending up a spray of dirt. Finally, he was through the fence and out of the camp. He ran until he saw a tank up ahead—a British tank. Ash hoped his worn-out clothes would let them know he was a POW and not a German soldier. A soldier near the tank pointed his gun toward Ash, who had his hands up.

The soldier put down his gun down and shouted, "Don't shoot! He's one of us!" Ash told the men where the Germans had positioned their tanks and guns in the camp. He also informed them where the prisoners were.

Soon, the Germans in the camp pulled out, leaving behind their prisoners. The British thanked Ash and gave him food and cigarettes.

"Boys," Ash said, "all I need right now is a little rest."

Chapter Ten

AFTER THE WAR

Bill Ash looked out the window of the plane and saw an airfield closing in below. *It seems odd to be a passenger and not the guy flying this bird*, he thought. The British plane he was in had taken off from Germany, which had surrendered just a few days earlier. It was May 1945, and the war in Europe was over. After more than one thousand days in POW camps, countless weeks in the cooler, and thirteen escape attempts, Ash was finally on his way home.

But after all these years away, where *was* home? Would he go back to Texas? Canada? Or settle in England? Ash decided to stay in England. He

had made friends with many pilots in the RAF, and some were lucky enough, like him, to have survived the war. One of them was his first escape partner, Paddy Barthropp.

When he arrived in London, Ash was able to track down his old friend. They met to discuss their futures.

"I'm going to stick with the RAF," Barthropp said. "I've had enough of combat, thank you, but they can always use good pilots to test new planes. What about you, Bill?"

Ash had been thinking about his future ever since the war ended.

"I think I'm going to go back to school," he said. "And I'd like to become a British citizen—if your country will take me."

Barthropp smiled. "After all you did to help us, I don't think that will be a problem."

Barthropp was right. The British government soon granted Ash citizenship. And he studied at Oxford University, focusing on politics and economics. He went on to become a writer, working as a journalist for a time and writing novels and plays for the radio. He also became active in politics, working for parties that tried to help the poor and average workers. Bill Ash died in 2014 at the age of ninety-six. He had lived a long and productive life. Newspapers in England and the United States reported on his death.

And they all described his adventures as one of the great escape artists of World War II.

AUTHOR'S NOTE

William Ash told his story as an escape artist in his memoir, *Under the Wire*. Other authors have written about the escapes he and others made while held in German POW camps during World War II. All of the events in this book actually happened, and the people mentioned by name are ones that Ash met during his time in the camps. Many of the thoughts Ash expresses in the book reflect what he wrote about his actual thoughts during his time as a POW.

In some places, however, I have created dialogue and some of Ash's thoughts, to fill in the details of his escape attempts. I have tried to remain true to the story of his activities as he described them and as they were recorded in military records at the end of World War II.

SELECTED BIBLIOGRAPHY

Ash, William, and Brendan Foley. *Under the Wire: The World War II Adventures of a Legendary Escape Artist and "Cooler King."* New York: Thomas Dunne Books, 2005.

Bishop, Patrick. *The Cooler King: The True Story of William Ash: Spitfire Pilot, P.O.W., and WWII's Greatest Escaper.* New York: Overlook Press, 2015.

Carroll, Tim. *The Great Escape from Stalag Luft III: The Full Story of How 76 Allied Officers Carried Out World War II's Most Remarkable Mass Escape.* New York: Pocket Books, 2004.

Doeden, Matt. *Surviving a World War II Prison Camp: Louis Zamperini.* Minneapolis: Lerner Publications, 2018.

Kogon, Eugen. *The Theory and Practice of Hell: The German Concentration Camps and the System Behind Them.* Translated by Heinz Norden. New York: Berkley Books, 1980.

Pearson, Simon. *The Great Escaper: The Life and Death of Roger Bushell—Love, Betrayal, Big X and the Great Escape*. London: Hodder & Stoughton, 2014.

Sullivan, George. *Great Escapes of World War II*. New York: Spectrum Literary Agency, 2012.

Willmott, H. P., Robin Cross, and Charles Messenger. *World War II*. New York: DK Publishing, 2004.

Wukovits, John F. *Life as a POW: World War II*. San Diego: Lucent Books, 2000.

Yomtov, Nelson. *Tunneling to Freedom: The Great Escape from Stalag Luft III*. North Mankato, MN: Capstone Press, 2017.

ABOUT THE AUTHOR

MICHAEL BURGAN has written more than 250 books for children and young adults, including *Who Was Theodore Roosevelt?* and *Who Was Henry Ford?* His specialty is history, with an emphasis on biography. His honors include the 2016 Carter G. Woodson Honor Book (National Council for the Social Studies) for *Shadow Catcher: How Edward S. Curtis Documented American Indian Dignity and Beauty* (Capstone Press). The book also received a Gold Medal from the California Reading Association. A graduate of the University of Connecticut with a degree in history, Burgan is also a produced playwright and the editor of *The Biographer's Craft*, the newsletter for Biographers International Organization. He first started writing for children as an editor at *Weekly Reader* before beginning his freelance career in 1994. He lives in Santa Fe, New Mexico.

ABOUT THE EDITOR

MICHAEL TEITELBAUM has been a writer and editor of children's books for more than twenty-five years. He worked on staff as an editor at Golden Books, Grossett & Dunlap, and Macmillan. As a writer, Michael's fiction work includes *The Scary States of America*, fifty short stories—one from each state—all about the paranormal, published by Random House, and *The Very Hungry Zombie: A Parody*, done with artist extraordinaire Jon Apple, published by Skyhorse. His nonfiction work includes *Jackie Robinson: Champion for Equality*, published by Sterling; *The Baseball Hall of Fame*, a two-volume encyclopedia, published by Grolier; *Sports in America, 1980-89*, published by Chelsea House; and *Great Moments in Women's Sports* and *Great Inventions: Radio and Television*, both published by World Almanac Library. Michael lives with his wife, Sheleigh, and two talkative cats in the beautiful Catskill Mountains of upstate New York.

Turn the page for a sneak peek at the next
GREAT ESCAPES ADVENTURE!

Chapter One

A HARSH REALITY

Eliza Harris pressed her body against the house.

Winter air chilled her skin. The conversation she overheard chilled her soul.

"He is willing to pay top dollar," said the voice belonging to Ainsley Seldon. "That little boy, Harry, plus a few others, gonna bring in the money I need."

Eliza felt as if an icicle was being shoved directly into her heart.

Mr. Seldon was selling a baby. A boy.

Her son!

Eliza was a slave. Mr. Seldon was her master, which meant he owned Eliza, her husband, and their son, the same as if they were horses or shoes. Slaves were not treated like human beings. As a young enslaved woman, Eliza was forced to live apart from her husband because that was how Mr. Seldon wanted it.

She had already buried two children—both died of pneumonia. The idea of losing another son because of the evil practice of slavery was more than she could bear.

Rage bubbled inside her.

She clenched her hands into fists.

Glancing upward, Eliza saw the evening sun painting the Kentucky sky a deep fire orange. Fat clouds laced with shades of charcoal gray approached as night began to fall. The scent of pine trees and winter snow filled her nostrils. Her breath came out in hard gusts.

In the distance, a wolf howled, hungry and prowling for its dinner. *Even he is free*, Eliza thought bitterly.

She attempted to move closer to the front porch where the men stood with their cigars—everyone knew that Mrs. Seldon didn't like the smell of smoke in the house. As Eliza stepped, a twig cracked under her foot.

The sound echoed like a gunshot in the night.

"Who's there?" said Mr. Morgan, Mr. Seldon's guest. Then footsteps, heavy feet on frozen snow. The men.

They were coming!

Eliza knew that if they caught her, she might get whipped to death before she could save her baby from the auction block. A slave found eavesdropping could expect punishment. She was in grave danger.

Looking around, she followed the trail back to the kitchen door. She heard the men's boots scrabbling over slick ice.

If she slipped on the icy puddles that coated the path, Eliza might fall and break her neck. Or worse. She could be discovered where she didn't belong.

The footsteps grew closer. Louder. If she could just make it to the edge of the house . . .

"Anybody back there? Ya better come on out!" called Mr. Morgan. He was a rough man with a

coarse manner. Eliza did not welcome the way he looked at her when he came to call on Mr. Seldon.

She dared not look back now.

With her heart pounding and muscles tight, Eliza made it to the corner. She threw herself against the back of the house.

Her body was shaking.

Not because she was tired. Not because she was cold.

But because she was angry.

She thought of her baby. Little Harry.

His faced popped into her mind and the image made her gasp. She wanted to hold him, kiss him, and stroke his hair.

Eliza and Mrs. Seldon had a regular nightly routine—Eliza would help get the Seldon children ready for bed as well as help their mother undo waist cinchers or difficult back hooks on her dresses.

Now all Eliza wanted to do was see her son. Instead, she heard her name being called. Mrs. Seldon's face appeared at the door.

"For heaven's sake, Eliza. You look like you've

seen a ghost. Before you go home, could you come inside again? Won't take but a minute. I need your help."

Eliza felt the rush of her own blood pounding in her ears. When she blew out a breath, great plumes of frosty air hovered before her face. There was always one more this or one more that. Always one more thing to keep her from her son.

Eliza tried to marshal her expression and extinguish the fire in her eyes. "Yes, ma'am," she said. Inside or outside, she needed to get away from Mr. Seldon and his rough visitor. She followed the lady of the house, helped the woman with one last task, then hurried away from the Seldons as quickly as she could.

Eliza moved swiftly but carefully across the icy ground. She was a young woman with golden-brown skin and thick, curly hair worn braided into a thick crown. She had never been extra girly. Instead, Eliza loved the outdoors. Loved the smell of fresh air and the sight of birds flying free in the sky.

And she loved the feeling of moving her body.

She had been a good runner when she was a young girl—just as good as any boy.

It didn't take long for Eliza to reach the small hill that led down to where she and the rest of Mr. Seldon's two dozen or so slaves lived. Within minutes she was at the door of Miss Sadie's cabin.

"How do, Eliza?" said the old woman who often looked after Harry. She sat in a rocking chair. A small fire burned in the hearth behind her. Wrinkles like lines on an antique map were etched into her dark skin.

She frowned. "Liza? What's wrong, child?" the woman asked.

Eliza entered the house and stopped, standing in the doorway, staring down at her baby. Harry was almost two. He had fat cheeks and wide, dark eyes. His tiny hands reached toward the ceiling of the old shack.

Again the older woman asked, "Liza? You come on in here and sit. You letting out all my warmth. What's got into you? Look like you done seen a fright."

After a moment more, Eliza collapsed to her

knees in front of Miss Sadie's rocker. She scooped Little Harry into her arms and held him tight. The baby fussed and giggled. His woolly head of glorious kinky hair tickled her face.

Her heart burned with love and pride.

Finally, when she had absorbed every bit of him that she could, she pulled away enough to look at the older woman. Miss Sadie continued to stare at her with concern.

"He wants to sell my baby!" she cried.

"Who?" asked Miss Sadie.

"Mr. Seldon. He was talking to Mr. Morgan after dinner, smoking their cigars on the porch like usual. I overheard him. He wants to sell Harry."

Miss Sadie gave a quick nod of understanding. Then slowly she shook her head. She had been a slave since she was a girl. She had witnessed so many families torn apart—one person sold to one family, while the wife, brother, sister, or child was sold to another—that she had simply lost count.

"It's our burden to bear, child. I'm so sorry," she said.

Eliza's eyes burned with fire to match the flames in the hearth.

"I will never let that happen!" she said. "Ain't nobody selling my baby!"

Miss Sadie was shocked by the young woman's words and look of determination. "Try to keep yourself calm, Liza. Won't do you no good getting in trouble for something you cannot control."

Eliza, however, was not about to calm down. She thanked Sadie, as usual, for keeping an eye on Harry. Then she took Harry and went to the cabin she shared with Miss Mattie, another old slave woman. Miss Mattie was such a good cook that the Seldons hired her out sometimes.

A surprise awaited Eliza inside—her husband.

"George!" she said.

Balancing Baby Harry, swaddled in a bundle of cloths, Eliza rushed toward him.

"It's the middle of the week. You don't normally come 'round till Sunday," she said, giving him a tight hug.

He held her, then stepped back and took the baby out of her arms.

George Harris cuddled his son, then stared long and hard at his faithful wife. Eliza sensed something was not right.

He edged her toward the far side of the tiny cabin. Miss Mattie said her how-dos and left, sensing the couple needed privacy.

Once they were alone, George let out a deep breath and bent to one knee so he could look into his wife's eyes. Eliza sat on a rickety wooden chair near the hearth. He placed their son in her arms.

"What?" she said.

"I'm leaving tonight," he said. "They sending me and Amos on an errand. Only this time, we ain't coming back. We just gonna keep on walking. It'll take 'em at least a week to realize."

"No!" she said, shooting to her feet. Her husband straightened.

"Let me finish, Eliza," he pleaded. "I know it'll be hard. But I've met some people. Good people nearby. People with connections to freedom. They gonna help us get to Canada. And after I get situated, I'll come back for you."

Eliza Harris, like every other slave in these parts, had heard many tales about the escape routes that came to be known as the Underground Railroad. It wasn't a steam locomotive that traveled below the earth. Instead, it referred to

hundreds of people—black and white—who provided shelter and guidance to those who wanted
to escape slavery or already had.

WHAT WAS THE UNDERGROUND RAILROAD?

All aboard! Next stop, freedom! The Underground
Railroad, a system of shelters and routes designed
to help escaped slaves travel north, began in the
late 1700s and continued through the Civil War.
Although the source of the name is unknown, it
is believed to have originated in the 1830s when
American railroads were booming. Rather than
being made of iron and propelled by coal, the
Underground Railroad used human ingenuity, black
people's knowledge of the landscape, and a variety
of transportation modes. Free African Americans
and whites worked together as "conductors," people
who hosted and led escaped slaves on their journeys
to the northern United States as well as Canada.

"George," Eliza said, "Mr. Seldon's gonna sell Harry! Our baby! I won't let him, George. I won't."

For a long time, George held his wife. He tried to console her, tried to assure her that it would be easier for him to find his way to the Underground Railroad alone and then return for her and Harry after he was sure they had a place to live free.

Even so, after he was gone, Eliza lay awake that night staring at the ceiling. She felt the warmth of her child pressed against her. In the dim light from the dying coals on the hearth, she made out rough shapes of scrap furnishings. Leftovers and hand-me-downs.

A terrible cold draft seeped between the wooden boards around her. With each harsh gust of wind, the small building seemed to sway.

Human beings ought not to live like this, she thought. Mr. Seldon took better care of his horses than he did his slaves. She pictured her husband disappearing into the night. The light of freedom leading the way like the North Star.

Her heart thudded in her chest. She feared it was loud enough to wake Harry. It was beating with the strength and courage of her ancestors. She'd lost her mother to slavery, having been separated from her years ago. She'd been a baby when her father was taken.

She squeezed Harry against her side.

"I won't let nobody take you, Harry," she whispered against his cheek. He cooed and turned over, nuzzling into her bosom. His softness and sweetness were enough to make her want to cry.

Eliza knew, however, that she had no time for tears.

It was time for action.

She would protect her baby.

Or by God, she'd die trying.